For Tara and Alexandra —K. H.
To Mary Craig with love —H. C.

LITTLE SIMON
An imprint of Simon & Schuster Children's Publishing Division
1230 Avenue of the Americas, New York, New York 10020
First Little Simon hardcover edition August 2020
© 2020 Helen Craig Ltd. and Katharine Holabird.
The Angelina Ballerina name and character and the dancing Angelina logo are trademarks
of HIT Entertainment Limited, Katharine Holabird, and Helen Craig.
All rights reserved, including the right of reproduction in whole or in part in any form.
LITTLE SIMON is a registered trademark of Simon & Schuster, Inc., and associated colophon
is a trademark of Simon & Schuster, Inc.
For information about special discounts for bulk purchases, please contact Simon & Schuster Special Sales
at 1-866-506-1949 or business@simonandschuster.com.
The Simon & Schuster Speakers Bureau can bring authors to your live event. For more information or to book an event
contact the Simon & Schuster Speakers Bureau at 1-866-248-3049 or visit our website at www.simonspeakers.com.
Manufactured in China 0620 SCP
2 4 6 8 10 9 7 5 3 1
ISBN 978-1-5344-6961-7
ISBN 978-1-5344-6962-4 (eBook)

Angelina™
and the
Princess

Story by **Katharine Holabird** Illustrations by **Helen Craig**

LITTLE SIMON

New York   London   Toronto   Sydney   New Delhi

Angelina was much too excited to sleep! The students at Miss Lilly's Ballet School had been asked to dance for Her Royal Highness, the Princess of Mouseland. Mr. Lightfoot, Director of the famous Royal Ballet Company, was coming tomorrow to help Miss Lilly choose the best ballerinas for the special performance. Angelina wanted a leading part so much that she worked on her pliés and pirouettes far into the night when she should have been sound asleep.

The next morning Angelina woke up feeling terrible. Her head ached and her ears buzzed. Angelina's mother took her temperature and shook her head sadly. "I'm afraid you'll have to stay in bed," she said. "You can't go to ballet school when you're not well."

But Angelina was determined to go. While her mother was busy downstairs, Angelina packed her ballet bag . . .

. . . and tiptoed out of the house.

Angelina arrived at Miss Lilly's Ballet School just in time to join her friends Flora and Felicity and all the other ballerinas who were waiting to go onstage. Flora did a nimble leap and a delicate spin...

. . . and then it was Angelina's turn to dance. Her heart
started beating like a drum, and she couldn't remember
what she was supposed to be doing.

The music started and Angelina knew she had to begin. She tried one step, she tried another...

...then she began twirling and spinning like a top until she was so dizzy she lost her balance, tripped on her pink ribbons, and tumbled down with a thump.

Flora and Felicity were given the leading roles in the
Dance of the Flower Fairies. Later, Miss Lilly called for
Angelina. "I'm afraid you will have to take a smaller
part this time," she said, trying to be kind.

When Angelina got home, her mother was very upset. "How could you run away like that when I told you to stay in bed?" she asked.

Angelina burst into tears. "I had to go to Miss Lilly's,
but everything went wrong. I did such a silly dance for
Mr. Lightfoot, I will never be a real ballerina! I am
not going to ballet school anymore."

Angelina's mother hugged her and kissed her and
carried her upstairs, and in just a minute she was
fast asleep in her own bed again.

The next day Angelina's headache was gone.
She felt better, but she was still very sad.
"It's not fair!" said Angelina.

"Maybe not," her mother said gently, "but things don't always go our way. You can still do your best with whatever part you are given, and that will help the whole performance."

Angelina thought about what her mother had said. Then she returned to Miss Lilly's after all, and rehearsed very hard with the other ballerinas for the Royal Performance.

After she had learned her own part, she memorized
the Dance of the Flower Fairies while watching
Flora and Felicity.

On the day of the Royal Performance, just as the show
was about to begin, Flora tripped and sprained her ankle.
Everyone was terribly upset.

Mr. Lightfoot and Miss Lilly turned to each other in horror. "Who can do the part?" they cried. Angelina was worried about Flora, but Susie stepped forward and said, "Angelina can!"

Angelina showed Miss Lilly that she had learned the
dance by heart. "But what about Flora?" she asked.

"Don't worry," said Miss Lilly, "we have a treat for
her. . . ."

So Flora was happy because she was invited to sit right next to the Princess of Mouseland. Mr. Lightfoot and Miss Lilly were happy because the performance could go on. Angelina was happy because she did the Dance of the Flower Fairies without forgetting a single step. The Princess of Mouseland was happy because she loved ballet.

When the performance was over, she congratulated Angelina and thanked her warmly for saving the show.